D0795392

OTHER OXFORD FICTION

Cool Clive, the Coolest Kid Alive

Two Books in One

Michaela Morgan

Illustrated by Dee Shulman

OXFORD
UNIVERSITY PRESS

OXFORD

UNIVERSITY PRESS

Great Clarendon Street, Oxford OX2 6DP

Oxford University Press is a department of the University of Oxford.
It furthers the University's objective of excellence in research, scholarship,
and education by publishing worldwide in

Oxford New York

Athens Auckland Bangkok Bogotá Buenos Aires Calcutta
Cape Town Chennai Dar es Salaam Delhi Florence Hong Kong Istanbul
Karachi Kuala Lumpur Madrid Melbourne Mexico City Mumbai
Nairobi Paris São Paulo Singapore Taipei Tokyo Toronto Warsaw

with associated companies in Berlin Ibadan

Oxford is a registered trade mark of Oxford University Press
in the UK and in certain other countries

British Library Cataloguing in Publication Data available

ISBN 0 19 275070 4

1 3 5 7 9 10 8 6 4 2

Typeset by AFS Image Setters Ltd, Glasgow

Printed in Great Britain by
Cox & Wyman Ltd, Reading, Berkshire

Cool Clive

Chapter 1

Look at the other kids in my class.

They have the right haircuts.
They have the right clothes – the jeans,
the t-shirts, the caps and the trainers.

These are my friends.

They may think I'm not all that big.

They may think I'm not all that
bright. But I know I'm really cool.
The trouble is my clothes are just
not cool at all.

'So what. I don't care,' I say to myself –
but I do care.

'You can wear my cap for today,' says
my best friend – but it's not the same.

My mum says,

My friend agrees with her. And I know she's right too. It doesn't matter. It shouldn't matter – but it does matter to me.

I want to be like my friends.

I want to be cool.

In my mind I can see exactly what
I could look like.

And I say,  But she always says,

So I say, 'Can I have some t-shirts
like those?'

But she says, 'You've got plenty of your
cousins' old shirts that you haven't
grown into yet.'

And when I say, 'Look at those trainers, Mum. I don't suppose ...'

She says, 'I'm sorry, love. We just can't afford them.'

It seems that almost everything I have belonged to someone else before me.

And the fashions have changed a bit since my cousins were kids.

At school we all had to make up a rap about ourselves. This is mine:

Don't have the right sort of trainers
Don't have the right sort of hair
Don't have the right sort of labels
Pretend that I don't care.

BUT
Oh **WOW!**
Look at them now!
All the style
All the know-how –
Puma, Hi-tech and Reebok,
Cool as Cool
They've got the lot!

And
Oh **WOW!**
I'm feeling green
They're the coolest kids
I've ever seen.
They're cool in school
and cool in the street
Cool as cool from
head to feet.

My friend says

It's a
good
rap.

But it's not such a good feeling.

7

Chapter 2

I know exactly what I want. I've seen them in a shop window.

And I know exactly what my mum will say:

Money doesn't grow on trees you know.

We don't have money to burn!

Maybe for Christmas...

I dream about those trainers.

Maybe I could find some long lost treasure and buy them.

Maybe I could earn a reward and buy them.

Maybe I could get a job and ...

That's what I'll do!

I'll earn lots of money and buy my trainers.

It's not easy finding a job, especially when you're my age.

First I looked at the newspaper.

SITUATIONS VACANT

WANTED
Hairdresser's
Assistant
Suit
School-Leaver
Phone: FAY 16841

SECRETARY
Mature
lady
preferred
Tel. 42136

GARDENER NEEDED
Suit Old-Age Pensioner
APPLY PO BOX 143

WANTED
Shop Assistant
Saturday work
only
AGE 16+
Tel. 41360

SALESMAN/WOMAN
Experienced
sales staff
required
PHONE 813

BUS DRIVERS
If you have good driv
ills apply to join our
m. PHONE REG. 41311

EXPERT SER

HYPNOTIST
Give up food
& smoking
Madame Gobb
Phone 31400

PLUMBER
Fix it Fa
Call Paul

They were all jobs for grown-ups or older kids. No good for me. What could I do?

I thought...

... and thought and ...

... I had an idea.

I could look at the cards in the window of the corner shop.

There were plenty of cards:

For Sale

Table Tennis Table by family moving house with slightly wobbly legs.

Tel. 33451

3 Adorable baby rabbits for sale.

Only £5 each.

Phone 42213 after 6

Typewriter for sale
Perfect working order
No good offers refused.

Phone 23%79$!

NEWSPAPER DELIVERY BOYS AND GIRLS WANTED.

APPLY WITHIN

That's the one for me!

I'll get a job, save the money, and
I'll be Cool Clive
The Coolest Kid Alive.

But when I asked, the man said,

You're not
big enough ...
not old enough ...
not strong enough ...
Come back when
you're older.

13

Outside the shop I met Rick Hamley from Mr Jacob's class. He had a newspaper round. He was dragging the bag behind him, and he was looking hot and tired.

I'm looking for a partner — share the work, share the money, OK? Tell your Mum I'll look after you. Start tomorrow. 6.30.

6.30?
6.30!
Surely he didn't mean 6.30 in the morning!!!!
He did!

That night I was so excited I could hardly sleep. I'd asked my mum if I could help Rick with his paper round and, after a bit, she had agreed.

She helped me set the alarm clock for half past five and she made me go to bed extra early.

It's hard to go to sleep when it's still light. All my plans were racing through my head. They made a sort of song which went round and round and round ...

In the end I fell asleep, and then

It was time to get up and get started on my first week delivering the papers with Rick.

MONDAY
was very wet.

TUESDAY
was no better.

WEDNESDAY
was worse.

THURSDAY
was even wetter.

But I carried on ...

On SUNDAY the newspapers are very thick and heavy.

I heaved that bag.

I hauled that bag.

I nearly gave up, but I carried on and I got paid. YIPPEE!

But the next day I met Rick...

19

21

Chapter 3

I went home and counted my money.

I made a special savings book and then I had a rest.

I was worn out and fed up and I still needed loads more money.

The next day I went back to the shop. I didn't go in, in case there were any more unhappy customers waiting for me, but I read the cards outside.

There were a few new ones.

For Sale

Set of Dining
chairs by
family moving
house with
solid wooden
bottoms.
Tel. 33451

10
Baby rabbits
£3 each,
for quick sale.

Phone 42213
after 6

DOGWALKER WANTED

Give my dog one good
walk a day, and earn
extra pocket money.

34 PARK WALK, BARKWOOD

YES! That's the job for me!
I wrote down the address,
asked my mum, and went around
to see the lady.

'You're not very old,' she said. 'You're not very big ... but you are the only one who's asked for the job ... so I'll give you a try.'

Here's his lead and here's ...

...Toodles!

'Now just take Toodles once around the park, then bring him straight back home. Don't get him tired. Don't get him dirty. Remember: once round the park and then straight back home ... '

She told me what to do over and over
and over again. I wish she'd told the dog.
Toodles had a mind of his own.
We went once round the park.
No problem.

But then
Toodles decided to go round again

NO TOODLES!

and again ...

and again.

We visited the ducks. Toodles liked
the water.

We visited the gardens. Toodles liked
the mud and the manure.

We visited the litter bins. Toodles liked the rubbish.

Then Toodles decided to go home – the short way.

The lady was not pleased. Not pleased at all.

She gave me the money for one day but,

I went home, counted my money, filled in my book, then had a bath and a rest.

From time to time I went back to the shop. Sometimes there were new notices:

For Sale
Baby's cot by
family moving
house with a
screw loose.
Tel. 33451

25 Rabbits
FREE
to a good home.
Phone or call
ANYTIME AT ALL
42213
47 Hutch Walk.

DUCKLINGS AND CHICKS
GOING CHEAP.
TEL 89136

But there was only one job:

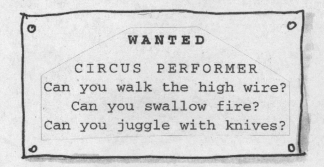

WANTED

CIRCUS PERFORMER
Can you walk the high wire?
Can you swallow fire?
Can you juggle with knives?

and that was NOT the job for me.

So I decided to start my own business.

I made posters:

and leaflets:

I borrowed some equipment –

a bucket,

a sponge

and a cloth

– and off I went.

I was doing very well, very well indeed, when...

...I had ... ...a bit of an ...

WOBBLE

A-A-ACCIDENT!

I was quite lucky really.
I didn't damage the car.
I didn't fall in the pond, but ...

I did break a few things.

I said 'I'm very sorry ...
It was an accident ...
I'll pay for the damage.'

And I did.

Now all I had left was my soggy
sponge, my cloth, and my bucket with
a hole in it.

Can you imagine how I felt?

I was trudging home by the park when I heard:

Toodles! Come back!

Then:

OW! KEEP THAT DOG UNDER CONTROL!

And then:

SPLOSH!

A crowd of people were gathered by the duck pond. I went to have a look and got there just in time to see a man crawling out of the water. He was wet and covered in weeds. He didn't look happy at all.

Gaz and Rick were trying to pull
Toodles away and apologize to the
man at the same time.

Chapter 4

There in the middle of the pond was his bag. It was bobbing about slowly and drifting around in circles.

'It's full of very important papers,' said the man. 'Oh no! It's going to sink! Get a fishing net quick!' he yelled.

But no. The bag was sinking and no one had a fishing net.

But I did have an idea.

I used my cloth, my bucket with a hole in, and a long stick, and ...

37

'Thank you. Thank you. THANK YOU!'
said the man. 'You've saved my bag and
all my papers and money. I would like to
reward you.'

He put his hand into his soggy bag and…	… I held my breath and wished.

Money? Money to buy my trainers?

Then he pulled out …	a little soggy card

	with an address on it.

'Pop in and see me,' he said.
And then he went leaving nothing behind but a patch of damp grass and some duckweed.

I went home and told my mum all about it.

So I had to wait till Saturday when she had the day off work.

In a way I was glad she'd come. It was a funny sort of place. It was a big warehouse in a side street, huge and dusty and full of boxes.

A bit spooky.

The man was busy telling me all about his job. 'I bring in all these things – some from other countries – and I sell them to shops.'

'I've seen some in shop windows,' I said.

'Help yourself to a few things then,' said the man.

'Oh we couldn't ...' said my mum.

YES WE COULD! YES WE COULD!

'Yes, you could,' agreed the man. 'Your boy saved me a lot of money and a lot of trouble. I want to reward him!'

So I got a cap and some jeans, a t-shirt and the trainers.

Cool!

In my new shirt I felt brighter.
In my new shoes I felt taller.
I looked the way I'd always felt I was –

Cool Clive,
the coolest kid alive!

So, Clive finally got his new trainers.
Read on to find out what happens
when Clive goes on a school trip in
'Clive Keeps His Cool' . . .

Clive Keeps His Cool

Chapter 1

Here's Clive.

Clive ran all the way to school.
It was a sunny day.
In fact it was:

Clive could feel the pavement heat
beneath his feet. He could feel the air
hot and heavy on his head.

Down the street he went.

puff puff
puff puff

Over the bridge he went.

pant pant
pant

Round the corner he went and...

← there was the school.

And there was the bus.
All ready to take Clive's
class to the farm park.

And there was his teacher, Miss
Strictly. She was holding the
register and marking it as everyone
got on.

Clive could see Barry and Gary,
and Sally and Sue, Dilip and
David, Debjani too and Joanne
and some others, plus a few
helpful mothers and one or two
teachers too.

Yes, they were all there and
they were all getting on
the bus.

'Hey, wait for me,'
yelled Clive.

Where's Clive?

But then the bus doors closed.
The bus engine revved up.
No one heard him... and
the bus pulled away.

Chapter 2

Clive stood on the corner. He felt like crying. What should he do?

Should he go into school?

Should he go back home?

Should he stay where he was?

What could he do?

It looked like Clive was…

…out of breath,	out of luck and…	…up to his neck in
		 TROUBLE

Or was he?

He watched the bus
pulling away.
He heard the children
give a goodbye cheer
and then…

...the bus made a funny little HICCUP and a splutter and... SSSTOPPED

The doors opened and the driver and Miss Strictly got out. Miss Strictly was getting cross.

'Don't you worry,' said the driver. 'This old bus won't let us down. It's just not used to the heat, that's all. I'll give it a drop of water and we'll be off.'

No problems.

Clive took his chance.
He sprinted forward
and slid onto the bus.

Cool as a cat, he plumped himself
down on the front seat.

Miss Strictly was still sighing and
tut-tutting as she got back
on the bus.
She settled
back into
her seat.

Unfortunately it was the same seat
Clive had just plumped himself down on.

It was difficult to
tell who screamed
the loudest.

It could have been
Clive.

It could have
been the other
children.

But it was probably Miss Strictly. She shot straight up in the air, hit her head on the roof, and then turned to see what she'd sat on.

Sorry, Miss—

Accident, Miss.

Clive blushed.

He moved to the back of the bus and squeezed in next to his friends.

Come on Clive!

The engine revved again. The bus moved away and everyone cheered.

HOORAY!

We're off!

— Again!

Chapter 3

Dilip and David explored their packed lunches. Clive explored *his* packed lunch. It had been a bit squashed by Miss Strictly sitting on it.

He tried to punch it back into shape.

The crisps and the chicken were a bit **flat**

and the biscuits were in tiny little crumbs

Luckily, not even Miss Strictly could completely flatten a can of cola.

Clive was hot after all that running.

He needed a drink.

He pulled the ring to open the can.

Now you know what happens to fizzy drinks if you shake them up and down, don't you?

You know what happens to fizzy drinks when you run about with them, don't you?

You know what happens if you open a can of shaken up and down fizzy drink on a bus?

It happened.

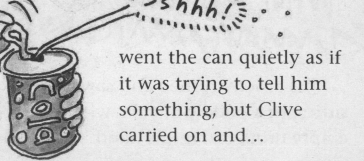

Sshhh!

went the can quietly as if it was trying to tell him something, but Clive carried on and...

whoosh!

... the fizzy drink exploded.

What was that?

Miss Strictly turned and saw Clive sitting in a puddle of cola, with an empty drink can in his hand.

The last drops of his drink
dripped off the end of his nose.

Was it you,
Clive?

Clive could not
deny it.

Miss Strictly sighed.

It looks
as if you can't
do anything
right today.

Sit next to me for
the rest of the
journey.

Clive went up to the front.
Everyone stared at him.
Sally giggled.

Gary laughed
as Clive
squelched
by him.

Clive felt hotter than ever.
He was stickier than ever.
He was thirstier than ever.
And now he had no drink
left.

Chapter 4

It was stuffy on the bus.

I'm sticky.
I'm hot.
Cool I am not.

CONTROLLING CHILDREN BY I. WACKEM

The back of Clive's legs stuck to the seat, but even so Clive sat still and quiet and good next to Miss Strictly. Behind him Sally started singing.

Everyone joined in, except Gary. He was busy eating. He'd got through:

a CHOCCO bar

two buns

his TANGY

and

...a bag of CRISPS

CHOMP

before Miss Strictly spotted him.

Gary never touched his sandwiches.
He always swopped them for someone
else's crisps.

Sally and her group were singing.

But after they'd got to twenty-two
men and their dog went to mow a
meadow, they stopped.

Joanne said,

Singing's boring.

'This is the *real* countryside,' said Miss Strictly.

But, after a while, nearly everyone agreed with Joanne.

But the bus rolled on and on and on...

Chapter 5

At last they arrived at

Miss Strictly glared at everyone.

Everyone got out and s t r e t c h e d in their own way.

David dashed off to the toilets.

Sally skipped off to see the lambs.

Aaaah, cute!

But Clive had spotted something far more interesting.

An ICE CREAM van.

He raced — off and — queued up — in a very,

very,

very,

long

queue.

At last Clive got
to the front but
Gary pushed in.

Can I have
your Crisps?
Swop you!

Clive didn't want Gary to push in.
And Clive didn't want to swop his
crisps. A bit of a scuffle broke out
and...

POW

BOP! WACK!

...the ice cream man got cross.

You- get to the back
of the queue!

And so Clive was a bit late

... and a bit messy

and Miss Strictly was not happy with him.

Miss Strictly took a deep breath.

Now we can get started. Gather round and listen. Mr. Twaddle is going to tell you all about cows, sheep and goats.

Chapter 6

Everyone gathered round and looked
at Mr Twaddle. A few sheep and goats
gathered round and looked at the
children.

Ahem–

'Is everyone listening?'
said Mr Twaddle. Everyone
nodded, except Clive.

Clive licked his lolly.
It was cool. It was tingly.
It was orange. It was zingy.
It was... annoying Miss Strictly.

'Listen carefully,' she said.

No wriggling, no fidgeting and NO EATING!

She glared at Clive as she said this.

So Clive stood as still and quiet as he could. He listened very carefully and held his lolly tightly behind his back.

But although he tried his best he couldn't stand very still when someone was *Pushing* and *shoving* behind him.

71

Clive did his best, but he couldn't keep absolutely quiet when he felt a funny wet tickling on his hand.

Clive did his very best, but he couldn't help fidgeting and wriggling just a little bit as he felt more and more tickling on his hands.

And he couldn't help giggling when he saw
Gary and Sally giggling and sniggering too.

Clive waited as long as he could but he couldn't help trying for a quick lick of his lolly when no one was looking.

Unfortunately he couldn't help yelling out

when he saw...

...a lolly stick.

That was all that was left of his ice lolly.

A small goat licked its lips.

It moved towards the lolly stick.
It wanted to eat the stick too!

Mr Twaddle shooed it away.

Clive stood and stared at his lolly stick.

It was the sort of lolly stick that had a joke written on it, but it didn't cheer him up much.

He looked so fed up that even Miss Strictly felt sorry for him.

We'll get you another – Now where's that ice cream van?

'Never mind, Clive,' said David.

But Clive did mind. He minded
very much indeed.

Chapter 7

'Cheer up!' said David. 'You can read us the joke on your stick.'

Clive sighed and did as he was told.

The others knew the answer and they knew some more animal jokes.

How does a duck with no nose smell?
Terrible!
Why do cows have horns?
Because their bells don't work!
What do you get if you cross a cow and a sheep and a baby goat?
The Milky Bar kid!
CHOMP!
CHOMP!
What's green with hairy legs and stingers?
I don't know...
Neither do I - but one's just gone down your neck!

How are goats like naughty kids?

'Cos they eat your lollies?

'Cos they keep butting in!

Clive thought of a new joke.
It wasn't actually about animals
but it was a good joke.

What football team sounds like an ice-cream?

Aston Vanilla!

So they all had a good time
until Joanne said...

Jokes are boring!

Chapter 8

Miss Strictly said, 'Time to fill in your question sheets.'

Clive was determined to do well.

So even when Gary was larking about,

Clive worked hard on his question sheet.

Even when Sally was chased by a sheep...

Clive worked hard on his question sheet.

And even when that goat tried to eat his shoelaces,

Clive worked hard on his question sheet.

He'd filled in all the gaps, answered all the questions and drawn rather a good duck.

So it was a pity his paper got...

...a little bit torn and messy.

And Miss Strictly was not pleased with him after all.

Then she said, 'Back on the bus everyone. We don't want to be late home.'

Chapter 9

The bus was hotter than ever. It had been standing in the sun all day long.

Clive shouted as he sat down on the hot seat.

While everyone else was singing or playing 'I Spy', Clive kept a lookout for the ice cream van.

But Miss Strictly said, 'Certainly not! We're all tired and hot and sticky and we want to get home.'

No one was tireder, or hotter, or stickier than Clive. And certainly no one was thirstier. But on they went until the bus started...

...hissing and steaming, made a funny little hiccup and a splutter. WHOOSH KERPLUNK Hissssss...

And then it stopped.

'No,' explained the driver. 'It's such a hot day the *engine* has overheated. I'll have to get some water. I'll walk to a petrol station. You all stay on the bus. I should be about an hour... or so...'

The children groaned.

The helpful mothers groaned.

Even Miss Strictly groaned.

Then... 'I've got an idea,'
said Clive.

Chapter 10

Miss Strictly gave Clive permission to take the driver back to the ice cream van.

The sun beat onto the windows of the bus. Miss Strictly sighed. Everyone sighed.

She and everyone else waited in the stuffy bus

They shuffled.

They waited.

They wilted.

They watched.

And then...

♪ Da da da dada da DA!!!

...over the hill came the ice cream van.

'Thank heavens,' said the helpful mothers.

'Thank Clive,' said Miss Strictly.

'Now I'll just get you that water,'
said the ice cream man.

'First things first,' said Miss Strictly.
'I want to buy everyone a nice cool ice
lolly. You all deserve one...'

All except Clive.

Clive doesn't deserve one.

He deserves two.

HOORAY!!
Everyone cheered –
except for Clive.

Clive was too busy licking his

ice-cold nice-cold tangy fruity fresh fantastic ice lolly!!

Chapter 11

So at the end of the day everyone got home safely and no one was late – thanks to Clive. And Miss Strictly and all Clive's friends got together and made him a 'thank you' song.

Other books you might enjoy:

How to Survive Summer Camp
Jacqueline Wilson
ISBN 0 19 275019 4

Typical! Mum and Uncle Bill have gone off on a swanky honeymoon, while Stella's been dumped at Evergreen Summer Camp. Guess what? She's not happy about it!

Things get worse. Stella loses all her hair (by accident!), has to share a dorm with snobby Karen and Louise, and is forced into terrifying swimming lessons with Uncle Pong! It looks as if she's in for a nightmare summer—how can Stella possibly survive?

A Game of Two Halves
David Clayton
ISBN 0 19 275071 2

Two stories about two very different football teams. In *Okay, Spanner, You Win!* Del is a brilliant striker but finds being a star is not always easy. Joey, in *The Booming Boots of Joey Jones*, is the complete opposite! He'd do anything to be in the school football team, but he's a one man disaster on the pitch.

The Worst Team in the World
Alan MacDonald
ISBN 0 19 275072 0

Reject Rovers are about to make history, the worst kind of history. If they lose one more game they'll claim a place in the record books as the official Worst Team of All Time. Can Kevin 'Panic' Taylor transform his team of no-hopers before Saturday?